For Claudia

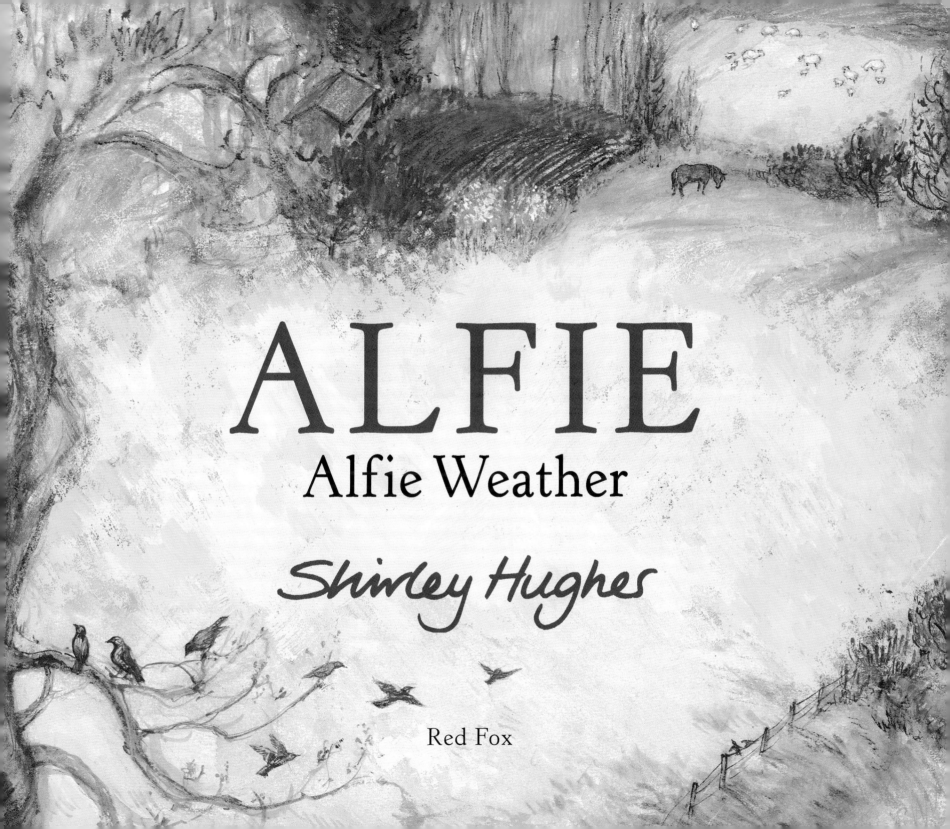

ALFIE

Alfie Weather

Shirley Hughes

Red Fox

Alfie Weather

Whether the weather is sunny
Or whether it's drenching with rain -
A river along the garden path,
A sea of mud in the lane;
Any old weather is Alfie weather,
He doesn't really mind,
Even the sort that nips his toes
Or the steamed-up-windows kind.
Sooner or later the clouds will set sail -
Maybe after tea...
Sooner or later the sun will come out,
And so will he.

A Journey to the North Pole

Alfie and Annie Rose and Mum were on a visit to Grandma's house. Outside it was cold and wet. Mum was upstairs doing some work on her computer. Alfie and Annie Rose were downstairs in the kitchen with Grandma.

Alfie looked out of the window. It was all steamed up. He could hardly see the garden outside. Raindrops trickled endlessly down the pane. He wrote an 'A' for Alfie on it with his finger.

Then he got down on the floor and started
to build a Space Station. But Annie Rose
kept trying to join in.

'Annie Rose keeps annoying and annoying
and annoying me!' wailed Alfie at last.
'She won't play with her own toys,
she always wants to play with mine!'

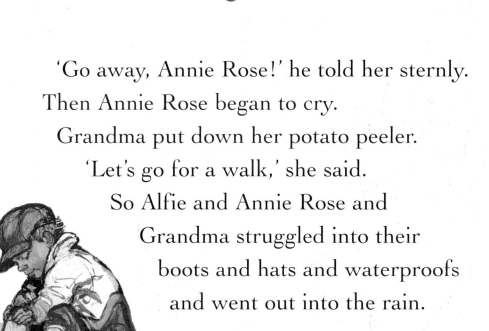

'Go away, Annie Rose!' he told her sternly.
Then Annie Rose began to cry.
Grandma put down her potato peeler.
'Let's go for a walk,' she said.
So Alfie and Annie Rose and
Grandma struggled into their
boots and hats and waterproofs
and went out into the rain.

The lane outside Grandma's gate had a stream running down the middle of it and plenty of mud. They held hands and slithered along together.

It was fun at first, sloshing about. But soon Annie Rose's boots were full of water.

Then she sat down in a puddle and got wet all over.
Alfie's feet were rather damp too.
They turned back towards home.

'What shall we do now, I wonder?' said Grandma when they were all dry again.
'It's not lunchtime yet. I think we had better go on an indoor expedition.' Alfie
wanted to know what an expedition was and Grandma told him it was a long
journey into unexplored territory.

   'We'll need supplies,' she said. She packed their little backpacks with some
crisps and bits of apple and four biscuits, and they set out.

They went all through the house pretending that each room
they visited was a different country.

They went through jungles,
where tigers prowled.

They swam in billowing oceans…and crawled through dense undergrowth…

…and made boats to cross fast-flowing rivers.

They climbed up steep
mountain paths besides
rushing waterfalls, hanging
on to the rocky sides in case
they fell in. And when they
reached the top they pitched
a tent and ate their supplies.

At last they came to the steep little wooden stairs which led up to Grandma's attic. This was the highest point in the world.

'This is the North Pole all right,' said Grandma, shivering. It certainly was cold. They could hear the rain beating down on the roof. But there were so many interesting things there that Alfie and Annie Rose quite forgot they were at the North Pole.

They spent a long time
exploring in old suitcases
and cardboard cartons full
of things which had been
dumped down and forgotten.
  Annie Rose found some
picture postcards and a
box with ribbons and bits
of jewellery in it, and a
handbag and a big hat.
Alfie found a broken
anglepoise lamp and a set
of dominoes and a kite.

'Time to go back to Base Camp,' said Grandma.

'Let's take our treasure with us before we freeze to death.'

Grandma helped them take it all down to the kitchen.

It was *excellent* treasure.

It lasted Alfie and Annie Rose for the rest of the day until teatime, when the sun came out.

Taking a Bite

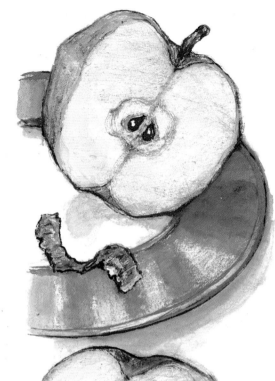

'Have an apple, Alfie,' said Dad.

It was a ripe, reddish green with a tight glossy
skin. 'I'll peel it for you,' said Dad.

And the peel curled into an S shape and a C shape
and a shape like a writhing snake.

'Here you are, Alfie,' said Dad.

And he cut the apple in half with a sharp knife.
Inside one half where the pips were snugly fitted,
a little worm was living.

It had scooped out a hole for itself and it was
alive in there slowly wriggling about.

'Yuck!' said Dad. 'Throw that one away and I'll give you another one.' But Alfie did not want to throw his apple away.

This was the apple he wanted, the one where the worm had made its home.

He showed it to Annie Rose. And they took it out into the garden and put it carefully down, so that if the worm got tired of being inside it could come out and wriggle about in the grass, just for a change.

Then Alfie bit into the other half and he thought it was the best apple he had ever tasted.

Alfie Upstream

One hot summer afternoon, when Alfie
and Annie Rose and Mum and Dad were
staying with Grandma, Mum and Alfie
decided to go exploring. It was going to
be just the two of them. Annie Rose was
going to stay behind in the garden with
Dad. They set out through the little gate
into the field. Jim Gatting's pig was lying
flat on its stomach under the big tree.
It was too hot to take any notice of them.
  They walked right across the field until
it began to slope steeply down to where
trees and thick bushes grew. Alfie had
never been this far before.

It was then that they heard the sound of running water. Alfie was very excited. They climbed under some wire and there, in the thick green shade, they found a little running stream.

'Now we're real explorers,' said Mum. The stream was shallow and had a gravelly bottom and floating weeds. Alfie and Mum took off their shoes and waded in. It was beautifully cool.

They splashed along. It was
very quiet except for the buzzing
insects and the sound the water
made. Sometimes they came to
some squelchy muddy bits and
sometimes a big stone in the
middle of the stream which they
had to climb over. And once Alfie
saw a dragonfly with shimmering
wings hovering over the surface.

Then they came to a place where
a tree had fallen down, like
a bridge across the water.

Beyond that the stream widened into a little pool.
It was deeper there. It came up to above Alfie's knees,
but he and Mum were brave explorers and didn't care
about a little thing like wet shorts.

They climbed on to the bank.
There was a smooth grassy space,
and in the middle of it a little apple
tree with branches which hung
over the stream. The apples were
still hard and green. They sat with
their feet in the water and threw
little apples in to see which would
make the biggest plop.

Mum stretched out on the grass. 'I think we've found
the Garden of Eden, Alfie,' she said sleepily. Right away
Alfie wanted to know what kind of a garden that was.

So Mum told Alfie the story of how,
at the beginning of the world when
all the plants and fishes and birds
and animals were brand new, there
were only two people on earth: a
man and a woman called Adam and
Eve. And they lived in a beautiful
garden called Eden and were free
like the animals.

   A river ran through the garden
and they had all they needed to eat.
But there was one fruit they were
not allowed to pick, and that was
an apple from a very special tree.

But one day the snake,
who was full of cunning,
told Eve to pick the apple.
Eve knew she shouldn't,
but she just couldn't resist
it. So she took a bite and
so did Adam. And after
that things were never
the same again.

Adam and Eve had to leave the Garden of Eden forever. They could never go back because the gate was guarded by an angel with a flaming sword. And from that day on they were no longer free like the animals. They had to work hard for their living.

'Like Dad and me,' said Mum.

Alfie thought about this. 'Well, I hope the apple was a nice juicy one, anyway, not all hard and green like these ones are.'

Just at that moment a very surprising thing happened.

Right in between where their feet were dangling in the stream a real snake, a little brownish green one, shot out of a hole in the bank. It wriggled out into the pool slipping very fast through the water, and disappeared under the fallen tree.

Alfie was too surprised to be frightened. 'Just like the story,' he whispered.

Mum said, 'It wouldn't have hurt us. It was too busy minding its own business.'

They sat there without talking for quite a long while until it was time to go home. And neither Alfie nor Mum ever forgot that time and that place.

Fox About Town

Sharp eyes, sharp nose,
Long bushy tail,
Pointed ears that miss nothing.

He's on the trail
Up by the wasteground,
Down by the railway cutting,
Ranging the edge of the playing field
Hunting for worms.

By day he's sunning himself
On the lean-to roof,
Or lying low under the shed.

But by night he's out and about,
Searching the rubbish bins,
Looking for titbits,
Chicken takeaways,
Fish and chips,
And the remains of school dinners.

Sometimes, under a winter moon,
You can hear the shrieking bark
Of a dog fox calling to his wife.

And on spring evenings,
In a quiet overgrown place,
Near the empty building site,
The fox cubs come out to play,
To frolic and bite
And pretend to fight.

Watch out for your rabbit!
Lock up your hamster!
No matter what people say,
The town fox is here to stay!

Winter Stars

Christmas was over. All the exciting parcels had been opened, and the Christmas tree, which had once been so fine and covered in beautiful sparkly things, was now waiting to be collected by the dustman.

But now something else nice was going to happen. Mum and Alfie and Annie Rose were going for a visit to Grandma's house. Dad had to stop behind and go to work, but he was going to join them for the weekend. It was dark when they arrived. Grandma was at the door to welcome them.

Alfie and Annie Rose were put
to bed in the little room next to
Grandma's. There was a door in
between which was always kept
a bit open. Annie Rose had a cot
in the corner and Alfie slept in
the wooden bed which had been
Mum's when she was a little girl.

That night Alfie lay awake until
very late. He could hear Grandma
moving about in her room. She
had put a night-light by the door
which made a pattern of stars on
the ceiling. Alfie lay and looked
at them until at last he dropped
off to sleep.

Next morning when he woke up
it was dark and the stars on the
ceiling were still there.

Mum and Annie Rose were asleep. So Alfie crept into Grandma's bed to keep her company while she had her early morning tea. They looked through Alfie's catalogue of beautiful shiny cars, talking in whispers and choosing which one they would like to drive.

After breakfast, when Alfie
and Annie Rose looked out,
the garden was all white
with frost. The trees and
bushes were just grey misty
shapes. It was too cold to
play out of doors, so they
stayed in the kitchen and
did some cooking.

Grandma was making
a pie for lunch. She gave
Alfie a lump of pastry and
showed him how to roll it
out on a board. You had
to put a sprinkling of flour
underneath so it didn't stick.

Then Alfie cut it into shapes
with Grandma's pastry
cutters. There were star
shapes and moon shapes
and round shapes
with crinkly edges.
Alfie liked the star
shapes best.

When he had finished he laid them carefully on a baking tray and Grandma
put them in the oven to cook.

Annie Rose rolled her bits into little balls and set them out
under the table for the teddies.

After lunch Grandma
and Annie Rose went
off upstairs to have
a nap. Mum and
Alfie went for a walk.
It was so cold that
both their noses
turned pink.

There were no
cows in the field.
Mum said they had
gone to live in the
cowshed where
it was warm.

The puddles in the lane were iced over. But it was thin ice and you could see the water underneath. Between the water and the ice were white frosty stars. The ice cracked and splintered when Alfie stamped on it. Then all the stars were gone. There was just muddy water.

Now the sky was turning pink too. On their way home, they saw one little star shining all by itself.

'Stars everywhere,' said Alfie.

When they got back the curtains were already drawn and Grandma and Annie Rose were getting tea ready, hot muffins and cake. They kept Alfie's delicious pastry stars until the last. They were just finishing tea when Dad arrived!

'We've saved you the stars,' Alfie told him.

'Good,' said Dad.

Then they all put on their warm coats and scarves and went outside. Now the trees stood out clear and black. You could see every branch and twig. And the sky was full of stars.

They all stood and gazed. 'You never see them like this in the city,' said Dad.

'How many stars are there?' Alfie wanted to know.

'Heaven knows,' said Dad.

Other titles in the Alfie series:

Alfie's World
Annie Rose is my Little Sister
Rhymes for Annie Rose
The Big Alfie and Annie Rose Storybook
The Big Alfie Out of Doors Storybook

The artwork for this book was painted in gouache colour and oil pastels and finished with fine brushes.
The picture of Adam and Eve expelled from the Garden of Eden is taken from Masaccio's fresco
in the Santa Maria del Carmine church in Florence, Italy.

ALFIE WEATHER
A RED FOX BOOK 978 0 099 40425 5

First published in Great Britain by The Bodley Head, an imprint of Random House Children's Publishers UK
A Random House Group Company

The Bodley Head edition published 2001
Red Fox edition first published 2002

12 14 16 18 20 19 17 15 13 11

Red Fox Books are published by Random House Children's Publishers UK, 61-63 Uxbridge Road, London W5 5SA

www.randomhousechildrens.co.uk

Addresses for companies within The Random House Group Limited can be found at:
www.randomhouse.co.uk/offices.htm

THE RANDOM HOUSE GROUP Limited Reg. No. 954009

A CIP catalogue record for this book is available from the British Library.

Printed in Singapore